Binkle and Flip Misbehave

Enid Blyton's Happy Days Series

Enid Blyton

Binkle and Flip
Misbehave

Text illustrations by Stephen Dell
Cover illustration by Alan Fredman

AWARD PUBLICATIONS LIMITED

For further information on Enid Blyton please contact www.blyton.com

ISBN 1-84135-218-7

Text copyright © The Enid Blyton Company
Illustrations copyright © 1999 Stephen Dell
Cover illustration copyright © 2004 Award Publications Limited
Enid Blyton's signature is a trademark of the Enid Blyton Company

First published 1938 by George Newnes
This edition first published 1999 by Bloomsbury Publishing Plc

First published 2004 by Award Publications Limited

Published by Award Publications Limited,
The Old Riding School, The Welbeck Estate,
Worksop, Nottinghamshire. S80 3LR

Printed in India

Contents

Chapter 1

Flip's Sunstroke

'Who's that coming up to the door?' asked Binkle, peering out of the window.

'It looks like a beggar,' said Flip. 'No, it isn't. He's got something under his arm to sell.'

Rat-tat-tat! The door-knocker made a terrific noise.

Binkle opened the door.

'Good morning,' said the visitor 'May I come in and show you my pictures? I'm Firky Fox, and I paint pictures with my brush. Beauties they are, too, I can tell you.'

Binkle didn't like foxes.

'No, you can't come in,' he said. 'Show me your pictures here.'

7

Firky held them out one by one.

'Oak Tree Town at Sunset,' he said. 'A very nice one, that. See the red sunshine on the windows! And here's Bracken Hill with the snow on it. A real beauty!'

Flip came and peeped over Binkle's shoulder.

'We don't want pictures, Binkle,' he said.

'Here's a nice one now!' said Firky. 'A field of turnips.'

'Yes, that is nice,' agreed Binkle, wishing it was real. 'I'll take that one. Yes, and I'll have this one too, with the cabbages and lettuces on a dish. And that one with all those hazel-nuts and acorns – and what about this one with the beetles and the cheese?'

'Oh Binkle!' gasped Flip in amazement. 'What in the world are you thinking of? You're not going to buy those pictures, surely!'

Binkle took no notice of Flip. He took out his purse, and counted out some money.

'There you are,' he said to Firky. 'I'll give you that for these four pictures.'

'Thank you,' said Firky, handing them over. 'They're cheap at the price!'

He packed the rest of the pictures under his arm, and went off, whistling cheerfully.

Binkle carried the four pictures indoors,

set them on the floor against the wall, and looked at them. Flip looked as if he thought Binkle was quite mad, and he rubbed his nose nervously with his paw.

'Do you feel quite well, Binkle?' he asked.

Binkle laughed.

'Yes,' he answered. 'And I haven't bought these pictures to hang up. Oh no, Flip! I've got a better idea than that.'

Flip groaned. 'What is it?' he asked. 'I shouldn't think we've got a single penny left after you've paid Firky Fox.'

'We haven't!' said Binkle cheerfully. 'But we're going to make *lots* of money with the help of these pictures.'

'How?' asked Flip curiously.

'Like this!' laughed Binkle, and picked up a piece of white chalk. He knelt on the floor and wrote with it. Then he sat down by the pictures, looking thoroughly miserable, and held out his cap.

ALL MY OWN WORK.
PLEASE SPARE A COIN TO KEEP
ME AND MY OLD FATHER

was what he had written on the floor.

'Oh!' gasped Flip. 'Binkle, you are dreadful! Whatever will you do next?'

'Any amount of things!' said Binkle, with a grin. 'First, I'm going to take these to Bracken Hill Town, where we're not well known. I'm going to find a nice sunny corner and sit down by my pictures. I shall have such a lovely lazy day, and only have to count how many coins come rolling in!'

'But what about your poor old father?' asked Flip. 'You haven't *got* a poor old father.'

'Oh yes, I have!' chuckled Binkle. 'You're the poor old father, Flip. I'm going to wrap you up in a shawl and muffler, and wheel you down to Bracken Hill Town in a wheelchair. You can go comfortably to sleep all day, if you like.'

Flip wriggled his nose and thought.

'All right,' he said at last. 'There doesn't seem to be much danger in your plan. I'll come.'

The two rascals began to make ready. Binkle fetched an old wheelchair out of the shed, and cleaned it up. Then he wrapped Flip in a big red shawl, tied a blue-spotted muffler round his head, and put him in the chair. He placed the pictures on Flip's knees and started off.

Over Bumble Bee Common he went, pushing Flip along quickly. Bumpity-bump! went the chair over the bracken and heather, and shook all the breath out of Flip's body!

'Let me get out and walk!' he begged. 'I can't stand this!'

'You're not standing it; you're sitting it,' answered Binkle cheerfully, going faster than ever – so fast that poor Flip hadn't breath enough to say another word.

At last they arrived at Bracken Hill Town, and Binkle slowed down. He went down the village street, pushing Flip along, looking for a nice sunny corner.

'Here's one that will do,' he decided. 'It's sunny, and it's just near the market-place, so there'll be lots of people passing.'

He wheeled Flip to the side, and fixed the chair so that it wouldn't run down the pavement. Then he spread out his pictures, wrote on the pavement with chalk, sat down on a cushion he had brought, and held out his cap.

Binnie Badger came hurrying by from market, carrying a bag full of potatoes. She stopped and looked at the pictures.

'That picture of the beetles is very good,' she said. You're a clever painter. Here's fifty pence for you,' and she put it into Binkle's cap.

'Thank you, ma'am,' said Binkle.

'Thank you, ma'am,' croaked Flip in a very quavery old voice.

Then came Susie Squirrel hurrying to market to buy nuts for dinner. When she saw the picture of nuts and acorns, she stopped with a squeak of delight

'I almost thought they were real,' she said. 'They're just what I'm going to buy for dinner. Here's something for you,' and she threw a coin into Binkle's cap.

'Thank you kindly, ma'am,' said Binkle.

12

'What did she give you?' asked Flip in a whisper.

'Twenty pence,' answered Binkle. 'Sh! There's a lot of folk coming now!'

Bibs Bunny thought the turnip-field picture was wonderful and she gave Binkle fifty pence. So did Bobtail Bunny, her husband. Hickory Hare loved the picture of the cabbages and lettuces, and Mary Mouse thought the cheese picture was beautiful.

Soon Binkle's cap was jingling with coins, and he could hardly stop himself whistling merrily.

'Fine supper we'll have tonight!' he whispered to Flip.

'I hope we *shall!*' said Flip. 'You've got the best of things, I can tell you. I'm getting hungry, and my! The sun is hot! Can't I take off this shawl, Binkle?'

'Good gracious, no!' said Binkle sharply. 'Everyone will see you're not an old rabbit, then. And don't stick your ears up straight like a youngster. Flop them down over your nose, as if you were tired out.'

Flip did so, and heaved a great sigh. Sally Stoat, who was just passing, felt very sorry for him.

'Poor old fellow!' she said. 'I'm sorry to see you're feeling ill. I'll give a pound to your son, and perhaps he can buy you some medicine to make you better.'

She dropped a pound into Binkle's cap and went on her way to market.

'A pound! That will buy you a fine lot of medicine, Flip!' chuckled Binkle.

'You just try buying me medicine!' scowled Flip. 'Buy me some lemonade instead. I'm thirsty enough to drink a bucketful.'

'That's a good idea of yours,' said Binkle. 'I'll leave you here for a minute and go and get you something to eat and drink.'

'Don't be long,' said Flip.

'No,' promised Binkle, and off he went down the street to look for a lemonade shop.

Flip began thinking of what Binkle might bring back. He thought happily for about ten minutes, then he began to wish Binkle would come back.

He craned his muffled neck round to the left, and looked down the street, but he could see no signs of Binkle!

'Oh, dear!' he groaned. 'I did think he'd be quick. Ah! there's somebody! Perhaps it's Binkle!'

But it wasn't. It was Dinky Dormouse. She stopped opposite Flip's chair, and looked at him.

'So your son's gone and left you, has he?' she said. 'Well, I hope he'll come back. It isn't safe to leave an old fellow like you alone, in the road. Anything might happen.'

Flip began to feel alarmed.

'Whatever *has* happened to Binkle?' he thought anxiously. 'He said he wouldn't be long! And what can I do? I'm supposed to be an old rabbit, and can't walk. Folk would know we'd been playing a trick on them if I suddenly jumped out and went to look for Binkle. Oh, dear me!'

Still Binkle didn't come. Half an hour went by, and another half an hour!

Flip got more and more worried. He couldn't think what in the world to do. Folk stared at him in surprise, as they passed, and wondered why he was all alone. Flip couldn't bear it.

The sun got hotter and hotter, and he suddenly felt very sleepy. He struggled to keep his eyes open, but it was no good. They would keep shutting themselves – and in two minutes Flip was sound asleep, dreaming of lemonade and lettuces.

Presently Sally Stoat came back from market. She was very surprised to see that Flip was all alone.

'Where's your son gone?' she asked him.

Flip made no reply. He was dreaming hard.

'Where's your son gone?' asked Sally in a louder voice.

Flip went on sleeping.

Then Sally became alarmed, and bent over him. She saw his eyes were shut and she thought he must be ill.

'Poor old fellow!' she said. 'I think I'd bet-

ter get help. Maybe he's got a sunstroke, sitting here in the sun!'

She beckoned to Dinky Dormouse, who was on her way back home.

'Dear, dear!' said Dinky in alarm. 'He was all alone when I passed, about half an hour ago. Hadn't we better do something?'

'Let's wheel him over to Hanna Hare's,' said Sally. 'Perhaps she'll know what to do for sunstroke.'

So together they unfixed the wheelchair and pushed it up the street to Hanna Hare's.

'Whoever have you got there?' asked Hanna in surprise.

'A poor old rabbit with sunstroke,' explained Dinky. 'His son has left him, and we're afraid the poor old thing is ill. What do you do for sunstroke, Hanna?'

'We must put ice on his head and put him in a dark room,' said Hanna anxiously. 'Dear, dear, what a sad thing! But first we must unwrap him and get him out of his chair.'

All this time Flip had been soundly sleeping, and not even when he was being wheeled away did he awake. But when Dinky began pulling at the muffler round his neck, he woke up with a jump.

'Ow!' he said. 'Stop it, Binkle.'

Then he caught sight of Dinky and Sally and Hanna.

'Ooh!' he said. 'Am I dreaming?'

'No, no,' said Hanna soothingly. 'Not dreaming. We're just looking after you. You're not very well, and we want you to come and lie down.'

'Lie down indeed!' said Flip, pulling his shawl round him. 'I'm not going to get out of this chair, I tell you! Leave me alone!'

'Just let me unwind this hot muffler then,' begged Sally, trying to pull it off.

Flip knew what would happen if that came off, and showed him to be not an old rabbit, but a young bunny.

He made a growling noise and jerked his head back.

'I've got a terrible temper,' he shouted, 'so don't make me lose it! I'm a dreadful fellow when I'm roused, *though* I'm old. I *won't* have my muffler taken off!'

Dinky and Sally and Hanna looked at him in alarm.

'Yes, it's very bad sunstroke,' whispered Hanna. 'I'll get Hickory Hare, my husband, to come and hold him while I put some ice on his head. Stay here for a minute.'

She tiptoed out of the room and brought Hickory back with her. He held Flip firmly whilst Hanna tied a big lump of ice on his head. Flip was so hot that the ice melted and ran in little cold streams down his neck. It was frightfully uncomfortable. But he didn't dare to struggle too much in case his shawl and muffler came off.

'Oh dear!' he thought. 'Why on earth did I let Binkle dress me up like this? I might have known trouble would come. Whatever *is* Binkle doing, anyway?'

Binkle at that very moment was hurrying back to where he had left Flip. He had gone to a greengrocer's and bought two fat turnips, which both he and Flip *loved* to eat raw; and then he had gone into a lemonade shop, sat down on a chair, and ordered two glasses of lemonade with parsley floating in it.

But when Rixie Rat brought it to him, he was fast asleep! He had put a pound out on the table, so she took it, and didn't wake him.

And when he *did* wake up, my goodness! he *was* in a state!

'Whatever will poor old Flip be thinking!'

he groaned. He drank one glass of lemonade, picked up the other, and ran off.

But when he got to his pictures. Flip wasn't there! Binkle rubbed his eyes, twitched his nose, and flapped his ears; but no, Flip still wasn't there!

'But where *can* he have gone to?' marvelled Binkle. 'The chair's gone too. It can't have gone away by itself. What a mystery! Oh, well I may as well drink this lemonade before I look for him!'

He drank it, and sat down to think.

'Flip can't be trusted by himself,' he said at last. 'I oughtn't to have left him. Perhaps he got tired and went home.'

This seemed to Binkle to be the only explanation of Flip's mysterious disappearance. So after a while he packed up his pictures and trotted off towards Bumble Bee Common.

When he got there he sniffed at the turnips inside the bag.

'Flip doesn't deserve any for scooting off like that,' he decided. 'And I'm hungry, so I'll just sit down here and eat them.'

He sat down and began munching, feeling quite sure Flip must be waiting for him at Heather Cottage.

But Flip wasn't. He was still in Hanna's sitting-room, getting in a worse and worse temper. He growled and fidgeted and flapped his ears and jiggled his chair until Hanna and Sally grew alarmed.

'I don't like it,' whispered Sally. 'Perhaps he's mad and hasn't got a sunstroke after all.'

'Perhaps so,' answered Hanna. 'What about fetching Wily Weasel over from Oak Tree Town? He'll find out where he belongs to, and take him back.'

Flip caught just two words of Hanna's whispering – and they were 'Wily Weasel,' the name of his enemy, the policeman of Oak Tree Town.

It was too much for Flip. He gave a terrified yell, leapt from his chair, and jumped straight out of the open window into the street! Up the road he tore, his red shawl flapping behind him and his blue-and-white muffler streaming out like a flag!

'Oh! oh!' shrieked Hanna and Sally and Dinky in fright.

'Oh, look at him! Look at him!' gasped Sally in amazement. 'Would you believe that an old rabbit could jump and run like that?'

'He *must* be mad!' said Dinky nervously. 'It's a good thing he's gone!'

'What a surprising thing!' said Hanna Hare, fanning herself and panting a little from the shock. 'I wonder who he is and where he lives?'

Flip tore on up the street, scaring everybody he met. He was dreadfully angry – angry with Binkle for deserting him, frightened that Wily Weasel might catch him, and terribly uncomfortable in his shawl and muffler.

He stopped when he came to Bumble Bee Common and began to unwrap his muffler.

Suddenly he heard a little humming sound near by. He peeped round a tree to see who it was.

It was Binkle – Binkle, eating a large turnip and humming cheerfully!

Flip was so furious that for once he forgot to be a meek little bunny, and he gave a tremendous yell and pounced on Binkle.

Binkle dropped his turnips and gave a howl of terror at the sight of Flip with ice on his head. Then Flip was on top of him and in two minutes he was thoroughly shaken and scolded.

'That'll teach you to leave me tied up in a wheelchair!' said Flip fiercely. 'Now I'm going to take the turnips and have a good feast by myself at Heather Cottage. *And don't you dare to come near till I've finished!* Oh! and here's a present for you.'

Flip took some ice from his head and slipped it down Binkle's neck!

Then the indignant little rabbit stalked off – and Binkle was so surprised that he didn't even dare to follow him!

Chapter 2

Binkle Tries to Be Funny

One day Flip came in from his shopping and found Binkle sitting in a corner of the garden with a wet towel tied round his head. He held a pencil in one paw and a piece of paper in the other. His nose was going up and down faster than Flip had ever seen it before.

'Binkle,' cried Flip, 'what's the matter? What have you got that towel round your head for? Have you hurt yourself?'

Binkle sniffed.

'Go away, Flip,' he said, 'I'm writing poetry.'

Flip sat down on the garden path in astonishment.

'Writing poetry!' he squeaked. 'I didn't

know you could. Anyway, what's the good of it, Binkle, and why have you bandaged your head?'

'Poets always do,' answered Binkle crossly. 'And I'm writing it because I've got an idea that people will buy my poems.'

Flip was so certain that they wouldn't that he got up and went indoors without saying another word. But as he was getting the salad ready for dinner, he began to wonder what Binkle's poetry was like.

He put his head out of the window.

'Hi, Binkle!' he said. 'Come and read me your poem!'

Binkle looked round and grinned.

'All right,' he said, and got up. He came indoors, and stood on a stool to read his poem. He looked very funny with the towel still round his head, and Flip wanted very badly to laugh. But he was afraid of upsetting Binkle, so he waited.

'Ahem, ahem,' coughed Binkle, pulling at his whiskers proudly. Then he began:

'To Dilly Duck
'There never was a nicer Duck
Than darling Mistress Dilly,

She's always most polite and kind,
And never rude or silly.

'Her beak is shining just like gold.
Her heart is golden too,
Oh, Mistress Dilly, there's no doubt
I think a *lot* of you!'

Binkle stopped.

Flip stared at him in astonishment.

'Oh, Binkle,' he exclaimed excitedly, 'fancy you writing that! It's *awfully* good. I've never heard better poetry, really I haven't! What are you going to do with it?'

'Send it to Dilly Duck with my very best wishes,' said Binkle, smiling in delight at Flip's admiration. 'I'll put it in an envelope now, and you can take it.'

Flip scratched his ear and looked at Binkle. 'But what did you write that about *Dilly* for?' he asked. 'I thought poets wrote about flowers and stars and things.'

'Well, I'll tell you,' said Binkle, busily pushing his poem into a very large envelope, and licking it down. 'Dilly Duck is very vain and she'll be so pleased with this that she'll show it to everybody. And *everybody* will want

poems written about them. And I shall make them pay fifty pence a time, and get a lot of money.'

'Binkle, you *are* clever!' said Flip. 'I couldn't have thought of that, and I couldn't have written the poems either, if I'd thought of the idea. I think you're a genius.'

'I think I must be a bit of one,' answered Binkle modestly, as he wrote Dilly's name on the envelope.

Flip ran off with the envelope and soon arrived at Dilly Duck's post office. He knocked at the door, and slipped the letter into the letter-box. Then he went away, chuckling to think what Dilly would say when she opened the envelope.

Dilly waddled to the door and took the letter from the box. Then she went back to her kitchen, put on her glasses, and opened the letter.

'To Dilly Duck,' she read.

'Bless my beak, it's a poem!' she cried in astonishment, and sat down excitedly in her big armchair.

She read the poem out loud all the way through. Her feathery throat heaved with excitement.

'Well, I never! A poem all about me, by Binkle Bunny. He's a bad bunny, but he's got a good heart, and he must be clever to write this about me! What *will* everybody say?'

She read the poem through again. When she came to the piece 'Her beak is shining just like gold,' she got up and looked at herself in the glass.

'Fancy him noticing that,' she said in delight. 'I must really have this framed. Dear, dear, dear, *what* an excitement to be sure.'

Dilly looked in her cupboard and found a little red frame that just fitted the poem. She proudly put it in, and then, going into her little office, she hung it up on the wall where anyone who came in could see it.

After a little while Mowdie Mole came in to buy a stamp. She saw the poem hanging in its frame on the wall, and bent closer to read it.

'To Dilly Duck!' she read, and looked at Dilly. 'My goodness gracious, who's been writing a poem to you?' she gasped in great surprise.

'Binkle Bunny,' answered Dilly, shaking her tail feathers in excitement. 'It's an awfully good poem, Mowdie, so true and so beautifully *put.*'

Mowdie read it through and turned to look at Dilly's yellow beak.

'Well, I never!' she said. 'I'd be proud if I had a poem like that written about me, Dilly Duck. Look, here's Sammy Squirrel from next door. Let's show him the poem.'

Sammy read it and was most astonished. He thought it very good indeed, and Dilly grew more and more delighted. Sammy said he'd fetch Herbert Hedgehog to see what *he* thought of it. He went out into the street to fetch him and brought back Riggles Rat as well.

Soon the shop was full of people reading Binkle's poem. Nobody there had ever tried to write poetry, and they thought it was simply wonderful.

Herbert Hedgehog took it down from the wall, sat down in a chair, and read it very slowly out loud. Then he said something that everyone else was thinking.

'Why did Binkle write this poem to *Dilly,* 'and not to anyone else?' he wondered.

Dilly looked a little offended.

'I suppose he likes me best,' she said, 'and anyway, I'm the only one with a beak. Perhaps *that's* what made him write it.'

By evening, everybody in Oak Tree Town

knew about Binkle's poem to Dilly. And everyone thought, 'I wish I could have a poem written about *me.*'

The more Mowdie Mole thought of it, the more she wanted one. And at last she determined to go and ask Binkle if he would write her one.

So off she trotted that evening, making sure no one was looking where she went. She soon arrived at Heather Cottage and knocked at the door.

Flip opened it.

'Come in,' he said, and Mowdie Mole walked into the kitchen, where Binkle was sitting with a towel tied round his head again.

'He's making poetry,' explained Flip in a whisper 'He says poets always have to sit with wet towels round their heads.'

'Fancy that!' whispered Mowdie Mole, all in a flutter to see Binkle making poetry, and wondering whether it was about *her* this time.

After a time Binkle sighed very deeply and looked up.

'Oh, good evening, Mowdie Mole,' he said. 'It's very, very kind of you to pay us a visit.'

'Well, you see, I saw that poem about Dilly Duck,' explained Mowdie Mole nervously. 'I *did* so like it. It was beautiful – and I wondered if you would write one for me, I *would* love it so!'

Binkle pulled his fine whiskers.

'Poetry's very hard work,' he said solemnly. 'I'm afraid I would have to charge you fifty pence for it.'

'I'd be glad to pay,' said Mowdie, putting her hand into her pocket and bringing up fifty pence. She put it on the table.

'Very well,' said Binkle, putting the penny in his pocket just before Flip got to it. 'I'll send the poem tomorrow. Goodbye. I can feel the poetry coming again.'

He made a face and groaned.

Mowdie Mole fled out of the room. 'I'm glad I don't write poetry,' she whispered to Flip. 'It looks as if it hurts dreadfully.'

No sooner had Flip shut the door than he had to open it again, this time to fat Herbert Hedgehog.

'Where's Binkle?' he asked.

'In the kitchen, making poetry. Sh!' answered Flip.

Herbert Hedgehog looked rather scared.

'I – I don't think I'll go in,' he said. 'Is it a sort of disease?'

'Yes, I think it must be,' answered Flip, thinking of Binkle's groans. 'He got it quite suddenly.'

'Well, I think his poetry about Dilly was wonderful,' said Herbert, 'but I don't think I want to catch the disease. Give him this pound and ask him to send me a poem about myself, will you? Don't tell anyone.'

Flip wriggled his nose and chuckled.

'I won't tell,' he promised, and let Herbert Hedgehog out of the front door. Binkle was tremendously pleased when Flip told him about the pound.

'I shall charge a *pound* for my poems, then,' he said, 'instead of fifty pence, as people want them so badly.'

He wrote the poems for Mowdie Mole and Herbert Hedgehog, and Flip took them round. They were both most delighted with them. Mowdie Mole's went like this:

> Mowdie Mole is very neat
> From her nose unto her feet,
> She has eyes so black and bright,
> They can pierce the darkest night,
> And her ears are nice and small,
> I think I like them best of all.

33

Herbert Hedgehog was so excited over his that he went down the street reading it out loud, so that everyone could hear.

> 'Herbert Hedgehog's a good old fellow,
> He lives in a house that is painted yellow,
> His prickles are long and sharp and brown,
> He's very well known in Oak Tree Town.
> He's rather fat and he's certainly funny.
> This poem is written by Binkle Bunny.'

He wasn't quite certain if he liked the bit about his being fat and funny, but he thought it was so lovely having a poem written all about himself, that he felt as if he couldn't mind *anything*.

By this time all Oak Tree Town was getting very excited over Binkle's poems. Everybody determined to get Binkle to write a poem for him- or herself, and Flip was kept very busy answering the door to people who came to ask for Binkle.

Binkle enjoyed it all immensely. He sat in the garden or in the kitchen, always with a towel round his head, because that seemed to astonish people very much. He had given up having it wet, because it gave him a cold and he found it hard to write poetry properly when he kept sneezing.

He was quite willing to write poems for anyone who liked to pay for them.

Nearly everyone in Oak Tree Town came and asked him for one, for nobody could bear to be left out. It became quite the fashion to have the poems framed and put up over the mantelpiece, and when you went to tea with anyone the first thing you did was to read the poem, and say, 'Very nice. Oh, very nice *indeed*'

One day Wily the Weasel came to Heather Cottage. Binkle was sitting in the garden as

usual with the towel round his head. When he saw the policeman of Oak Tree Town coming in the gate, he got up hurriedly and scuttled indoors. He wasn't at all sure whether Wily had come for a poem, or to scold him for something naughty he had done at some time or other.

But Wily had come for a poem. He didn't like Binkle for he felt he was a very bad bunny, but he couldn't bear to be the only one who hadn't a poem about himself.

'Hi, Binkle!' he called. 'Will you write me a poem?'

'Certainly,' answered Binkle, putting his head out of the window. 'That will be five pounds.'

'Don't be silly,' answered Wily. 'I'll give you fifty pence, and you'll do it for that, or I'll remember something bad you've done and come in and scold you. Here's fifty pence. Catch it.'

Binkle bristled his whiskers, caught the fifty pence piece, and wished he dared say something rude. A sudden thought came to him, and he grinned.

'All right, Wily' he called. 'I'll send the poem tomorrow.'

All that night he made it up and, when it was finished, he copied it out neatly. Then he crept through Oak Tree Town to where Wily Weasel lived, and pinned the poem up on the door. Then he ran back, chuckling.

When Wily Weasel was having breakfast next morning, he and his wife heard a laughing and talking going on outside. When he peeped out of the window, he saw a crowd of folk looking at something on his door.

'Come out and read your poem, Wily,' they called. 'It's a *lovely* one!'

Wily opened the door and saw the piece of paper pinned on it. This is what he read:

'Wily Weasel came to me,
Yesterday, just after tea,
And asked if I would kindly write
A little poem, nice and bright,
To say how kind he is, and wise,
And how we like his pretty eyes,
And how we'd love to kiss his nose,
And watch his dainty twinkling toes.
But all that I can *truly* write
About our policeman on this night,
Is how I hope he'll catch a measle,
For I don't like Wily Weasel!'

Wily Weasel was furiously angry. He knew that all Oak Tree Town would hear of Binkle's joke and enjoy it, and he tore the paper down, in a great rage.

He raced up to Heather Cottage, determined to punish Binkle. But Binkle was ready for him and the doors were bolted. Binkle poked his head out of the window.

'Have you come for another poem?' he asked politely.

'How *dare* you write like that about me?' raged Wily.

'Oh, didn't you like it?' asked Binkle in great surprise, sticking his big ears up

straight. 'Well, I didn't want to write it, you know; you made me do it. I can't help what poetry comes into my head, can I? You shouldn't have made me do it for you.'

Wily went off angrily, feeling it really *was* his own fault.

But, dear me, Oak Tree Town didn't bother at all about whose fault it was. They enjoyed the joke thoroughly and thought Binkle not only clever, but funny.

Binkle began to think he was too, and started writing funny poems that weren't very kind. Then things began to go wrong for him. It happened like this.

Oak Tree Town heard that Oll the otter, who was King of Runaway River, beyond Bracken Hill, was coming to visit Oak Tree Town. They were very excited about it.

'What can we do to give him a good welcome?' they cried.

'I know,' said Herbert Hedgehog, thinking of his framed poem at home. 'Let's get Binkle to write a poem about Oak Tree Town to present to Oll the otter. That will make him very pleased, and he will think what clever people we must be here. We'll tell Binkle to put in lots of nice things about us.'

'Good idea, good idea!' cried everyone, patting Herbert Hedgehog on the back till he choked.

Sammy Squirrel was chosen to go and ask Binkle. He set off that very evening and found Flip and Binkle both in the garden.

Sammy didn't take long telling Binkle what Oak Tree Town wanted.

'And mind you say lovely things about everyone,' he said, 'and you'll have two pounds.'

'All right,' said Binkle, very pleased. 'What will I get if I say things that *aren't* lovely, Sammy?'

'Nothing at all,' said Sammy crossly. 'So don't try any tricks like you tried on Wily Weasel, Binkle.'

Sammy went home and left the two bunnies alone. Binkle looked rather mischievous, and Flip began to be afraid he was going to do something naughty.

'Binkle,' he begged, 'tie your towel round your head and begin writing a *lovely* poem. Please, oh please, don't write anything bad!'

Binkle loved teasing Flip. He smoothed his whiskers and chuckled.

'Go away, Flip,' he said. 'I'll read you what I've written when it's done.'

Now Binkle meant to write a fine poem, but he also thought it would be rather fun to write a naughty one just to shock Flip. So he set to work on the two poems, while Flip watched him anxiously from the kitchen window.

When they were done he went indoors.

'Here you are, Flip,' he said, giving him the naughty poem. 'Do you think that will do?'

This is what Flip read:

'Your Majesty, please will you hear,
This verse by Binkle Bunny,
Who welcomes you to Oak Tree Town
And all its people funny.
Let me tell you who we are,
Here's a Hedgehog vain,
And here's a Badger and a Duck
Who're both extremely plain.
Then there's Wily Weasel,
How we wish he'd go!
Don't be friendly with him,
He isn't nice to know.'

When Flip had read as far as this, his knees began to shake and he sat down on a chair.

'Binkle!' he groaned. 'I can't bear it. It's unkind. We'll be turned out of Oak Tree Town.'

'The end's all right,' chuckled Binkle, twitching his ears in delight, and taking the poem from Flip. 'Listen!

> The only persons in this town
> Who're really worth your trip,
> Are Binkle, with his whiskers fine,
> And naughty little Flip.'

Flip would have torn up the whole poem if he could have got it, but Binkle wouldn't let him. So Flip went to bed very miserable, while Binkle stayed up and copied out his good poem in his best writing.

Oll the Otter was coming the next day and Binkle was to read his welcoming poem in the Town Hall just before the feast held in honour of King Otter's arrival.

When the time came, he dressed himself carefully, and let poor Flip into the secret of his other poem.

'The other poem's fine!' he laughed. 'You wait till you hear it.'

Flip was very relieved. He was never quite certain what Binkle would do.

Binkle stuffed his poem into his pocket and set off with Flip. They had just taken their places on the platform when Oll the Otter arrived, very pleased to find such a welcome awaiting him.

When he heard that a poem was to be read, he was still better pleased. He thought poetry was tremendously clever.

Binkle, feeling very important, pulled out his poem, and, just a little nervous, began to read it.

> 'Your Majesty, please will you hear,
> This verse by Binkle Bunny,'

he began.

> 'Who welcomes you to Oak Tree Town,
> And all its people funny.
> Let me tell you who we are,
> Here's a Hedgehog vain . . .'

Binkle suddenly stopped and gazed at his poem in horror.

He had put the wrong one in his pocket! Whatever was he to do? His nose twitched nervously and he blinked his eyes. Everybody stared.

'It's – it's the wrong poem,' he stammered at last.

'Oh, never mind,' said Oll the Otter graciously. 'I like any poetry, and I don't mind a bit what it's about. Go on.'

'I don't think I can,' said Binkle, pulling his whiskers so hard that one long one came out. 'The right one's at home. Flip, go and fetch it!'

'Well, while Flip is gone, read me *that* one,' said Oll the Otter, growing very curious to hear it.

There was nothing for Binkle to do but read it. He felt simply dreadful, for no one spoke a word all the time, and he was nearly crying when he reached the end.

'H'm, not very funny, and very unkind,'

said Oll the Otter. 'I think you deserve a scolding, and hope you'll get it.'

'He certainly will,' said Wily Weasel, coming forward and taking hold of Binkle by his collar. He was hurried out of the hall and locked up in a shed.

Flip soon came back, and Wily Weasel read the proper poem to Oll the Otter, who thought it very good.

'It's a pity he doesn't always write like that,' he said. 'I should scold him, but not too much. And I shouldn't encourage him to write any more. He can't be trusted.'

Then they all sat down to the feast and thoroughly enjoyed themselves; except poor Flip, who couldn't help feeling sorry for Binkle. He squashed a lettuce into his pocket to give him afterwards.

Binkle got his scolding, but not too much, and when he went home with Flip he felt very sorry indeed that he had been silly enough to spoil his day.

'If you hadn't tried to be too clever, you'd have been a lot happier,' said Flip, giving him his lettuce.

Chapter 3

'Swee-ee-eep!'

'Is there any food in the cupboard, Binkle?' asked Flip, opening one eye and looking at Binkle, who was dressing.

'No, there isn't, and you know that very well!' snapped Binkle, who was in a very bad temper. 'You just jump out of bed, you lazy thing. We've got to *work* today, if we want any food to eat!'

'Oh, oh!' groaned Flip. 'I do hate work! Whatever can we do, Binkle?'

'We must think,' said Binkle. 'Hark! Who's that calling outside?'

He went to the window and leaned out.

Brock Badger the Sweep was outside, carrying his poles and brushes over his shoulder.

'Sweeeep! Sweeeep!' he called, in his deep, husky voice. Then he caught sight of Binkle at the window.

'Chimneys swept, Binkle?' he asked.

'No!' answered Binkle, and Brock went off, crying, 'Sweeeep!' again over Bumble Bee Common.

Binkle watched him.

'Flip,' he said, 'come here!'

Flip came to the window.

'See old Brock!' said Binkle. 'He gets a good lot of money by sweeping chimneys. And there's nothing much in it! Just fix your poles together, swish the brush up the chimney, and there you are!'

'Sounds nice and easy!' said Flip, watching Brock Badger knock at Slippy Stoat's door in Briar Bank.

'It is easy,' said Binkle, 'and what's more, *we'll* do it, Flip! We'll borrow Brock's poles and brushes, and go off to Bracken Hill Town away yonder, and sweep all the chimneys we can! My! We'll come back with our pockets full of money!'

'But how can we get Brock to lend us his brushes?' asked Flip doubtfully. 'Nobody round here trusts us much, you know.'

47

'Wait and see!' answered Binkle cheerfully. 'Come on! There goes Brock over the Common. Let's catch him up.'

The two rabbits scurried downstairs and ran over the Common. They couldn't see which way Brock had gone, so Flip went down Heather path and Binkle ran down Hazel Road.

After a bit, Binkle smelt smoke, and he peered round a tree and found Brock Badger cooking his breakfast. It smelt very good. Binkle watched Brock with his bright brown eyes, and wondered how he could get him to lend his poles and brushes.

Brock finished his breakfast, kicked out the fire, and lit his pipe. He leaned back against a tree and smoked hard.

Gradually his eyes closed, his pipe fell from his mouth, and he began to snore loudly.

Binkle grinned. He knew how he was going to borrow Brock's brushes now!

He stole round the tree, picked up Brock's bundle, slung it over his shoulder, and ran off, chuckling.

'My!' said Flip, meeting him at a bend in Hazel Road. 'How on earth did you get Brock to lend you his things, Binkle?'

'He didn't say no, and he didn't say yes,' chuckled Binkle, 'so I just took them! He was sound asleep, Flip!'

'Well, we'll have to give them back when we've finished with them,' said Flip nervously. 'We don't want Wily Weasel the policeman after us, you know!'

'Stuff and nonsense!' laughed Binkle. 'Come on! We'll make a lot of money today in Bracken Hill Town, Flip. We'll give Brock a fine dinner for lending us his brushes, when we come back!'

Off the two went, and after a long walk arrived at Bracken Hill Town.

'Wweeeep!' shouted Binkle. 'Wweeeeep! Here, Flip! I can't shout and carry these things! You carry them and then I can shout properly!'

Flip took them, grumbling, and Binkle began to shout in a most tremendous voice.

'*Sweeee-eep! Sweeeeeep!* Twenty-two chimneys swept yesterday – what do you think of *that*, folks? Sweeeep! Finest sweeps in the world! Sweeeep!'

'Binkle! We'll get into trouble if you say we're the finest sweeps in the world,' began Flip hurriedly. 'Everyone'll *know* we're not!'

49

'Be quiet, Flip! How are they to know? And, anyhow, we *might* be the finest sweeps out! You can't tell till you've tried!' said Binkle in a fierce whisper.

Flip said no more, but followed Binkle, carrying the poles and very much hoping that no one wanted chimneys swept that morning. He felt extremely nervous about it.

Bushy Squirrel knocked at her window-pane. Binkle looked up and pulled his cap off politely.

'Sweep your chimney, ma'am?' he called.

'Yes!' answered Bushy. 'It's been smoking terribly this morning. You've just come along in time. But don't make more mess than you can help, will you?'

Binkle and Flip went into the little house. It only had one chimney, so they couldn't make any mistake about sweeping the right one.

Binkle began fixing the poles together, and pushed the first one up the chimney, with the brush fixed well on.

Suddenly the brush reached something hard and wouldn't go any farther. Binkle pushed and pushed, but it was no good.

He pulled down the brush and put his head up the chimney to look.

Then he reached his paw up and tried to feel what it was. It was a brick fallen down, blocking up the chimney so that the smoke couldn't go up properly.

Binkle twisted the brick about until he got it loose enough, and then, turning it sideways up, he neatly lifted it down the chimney.

'Say, Flip,' he whispered, 'this chimney doesn't need sweeping! This brick stopped it up!'

'Shall we go and tell Bushy Squirrel?' said Flip jumping up.

'Rather not!' said Binkle, scornfully. 'Pack up the poles and brushes, and leave this to me, Flip!'

Whilst Flip was busy tying up the bundle, Binkle got paper and wood and laid a fire. He lighted it, and when it was crackling merrily, with the blue smoke going up the chimney, he called Bushy Squirrel.

She came running in.

'Have you finished already?' she asked in surprise.

'Your chimney is perfectly all right now,' said Binkle, waving his hand towards the crackling fire. 'See, we have lit a fire for you to show you that the chimney doesn't smoke. And we haven't made a mess of your room at all, have we?'

'Well, well, well!' marvelled Bushy, holding her paws up in astonishment. 'Not a mite of soot anywhere, and all so quickly done too. You certainly *are* marvellous sweeps!'

Just then someone went by the window. Bushy ran to it and leaned out.

'Mary Mole!' she called. 'Mary Mole! Just come in here a minute and see what I've had done!'

Mary Mole came waddling in; and was delighted to see how wonderfully clean the sweeps had kept the room.

'My bedroom chimney badly wants

sweeping,' she said. 'Could you come and do it now? I was going to let Brock the Badger do it, but he is not as clean or as quick as you are.'

'Certainly, ma'am!' answered Binkle, shouldering his poles. 'We'll come now. We charge a pound, please, for sweeping chimneys,' he said, turning to Bushy Squirrel.

'Very cheap – very cheap!' said Bushy, feeling for her purse. Binkle wished he had said two pounds, but it was too late to change.

Then Flip and Binkle followed Mary Mole to her house in the middle of the village. She took them up to her little blue-and-white bedroom.

'Here you are,' said she. 'I *am* so glad I heard of you. Brock Badger always makes such a dreadful mess, though he *does* try hard not to. I have to cover up everything in the room with sheets when he comes!'

She left the room and went downstairs. Flip began fixing the poles together and Binkle sat in a chair near by and watched him.

'Up the chimney she goes!' he said. 'It *is* nice to see you doing some work, Flip. Push hard!'

The chimney was small and the brush Flip

had fitted on was very big. He pushed and pushed, and suddenly it gave, and slipped up the chimney with a rush, quite overbalancing Flip.

At the same moment a great cloud of soot fell down into the hearth and completely covered him. It flew all over the white room and settled everywhere. Binkle leaped up and began to choke and cough.

'You stupid!' he cried angrily. *'That's* not the way to sweep a chimney!'

'You should have swept it yourself, then!' choked Flip, trying to wipe himself clean, but making himself blacker still.

'Let's find the bathroom!' said Binkle. 'We

can't go out like this! No one will give us work!'

They went into the bathroom near by, and turned on the taps. But instead of making themselves clean, they made the bathroom terribly dirty. The bath was streaked with black, and the floor was covered with soot. When they dried themselves, the towels looked terrible with great black marks and smudges.

'Binkle,' said Flip, looking at his towel in dismay. 'Whatever will Mary Mole say! She *will* be angry with us!'

'This all comes of you trying to sweep a chimney!' scolded Binkle. 'Next time I'll do it. Look here, we'd better slip out of the house quietly when Mary Mole isn't looking.'

The two scamps tiptoed out of the bathroom, wrapped up their bundle of poles, and leaned over the banisters to see if Mary Mole was anywhere about.

'Listen! She's ironing in the kitchen!' said Binkle. 'We can slip out of the front door without being seen!'

So the two rabbits crept downstairs and slipped out of the front door as quietly as they could.

'Thud-thud!' went Mary's iron, and they heard her humming a little song. Poor Mary! Whatever would she say when she went upstairs!

Binkle and Flip went down the road very quietly, not daring to call out 'Sweeep!' until they were well out of Mary's hearing. When they had turned two corners and were well into an old part of Bracken Hill Town, they felt safer.

'Big houses here!' said Binkle, glancing round. 'We could get quite a lot of chimneys to sweep, I expect. Swee-ee-eep! Swee-ee-eep!'

A housekeeper mouse came running out of a big house and beckoned to them.

'Hi! Hi!' she called. 'Sweep! Sweep!'

Binkle and Flip went up to her.

'Oh!' she said, disappointed. 'I thought you were Brock Badger the Sweep. He was supposed to be coming to our house this morning to sweep the chimneys, and he hasn't come!'

'Can't we do them instead?' asked Binkle politely. 'I saw Brock Badger fast asleep off Hazel Road this morning, so I expect he's forgotten.'

At that moment the lady of the house, Binnie Badger, came out.

'Where's my cousin Brock?' she asked. 'I always let him sweep the chimneys because he's my cousin. Still, perhaps *you'd* better come and do it. If Brock can't remember, he must go without the job. Come along!'

She led the way indoors. Flip and Binkle followed, grinning at each other.

Binnie took them into the big sitting-room. Dust-sheets covered the furniture, and everything was ready for the sweep. She left them there, and they began to unpack the poles and brushes once more.

'I'm going to sweep the chimney this time!' said Binkle firmly. 'We can't have an awful mess like last time!'

'All right!' said Flip. 'I'm sure I don't want to sweep! It's a nasty, dirty job!'

He sat down on a chair to watch Binkle. Binkle was very busy. Up the chimney went the brush, and pole after pole was fitted neatly on. Soon there were very few poles left.

'I wonder if the brush has reached the top of the chimney yet,' said Binkle suddenly with a sigh. 'It's jolly hard work pushing and pushing, and it gets heavier each time I fix another pole on. How do you tell when the brush has reached the top, do you suppose, Flip?'

'I don't know!' said Flip. 'Perhaps, if I went outside and looked, I could see if the brush was sticking out of the chimney!'

'No, you mustn't do that!' said Binkle. 'Bushy Squirrel might happen to come along and see you, and then we should get into a row!'

He fixed another pole on and pushed. 'Oh dear!' he sighed. 'I do wonder if it's at the top yet! It would be *so* silly if the brush was sticking ever so far up into the air, wouldn't it, Flip?'

Then Flip had an idea.

'Can't I go up on the roof and see!' he said. 'I expect there's a skylight up in an attic somewhere that I can squeeze through.'

'Yes, that's a fine idea!' said Binkle, very pleased. 'Go on up now, Flip.'

So Flip made his way upstairs, and soon came to a little attic. In the ceiling was a slanting skylight. Flip put a chair underneath, stood on it, and opened the skylight. Then he climbed through it, and there he was, on the roof.

'Goodness!' said Flip, holding on to a chimney near by. 'What a lot of them! Now I wonder which chimney Binkle's sweeping.'

He looked carefully all round. None of the chimneys seemed to have a brush sticking out.

'That's a funny thing!' said Flip. 'I suppose Binkle's not made the brush long enough yet. Well, I'll sit down and wait till I see the brush come out, and then I'll go down and tell him.'

He sat down by a chimney and waited. it was very dull. Soon he stopped watching the chimneys and looked away over the country. There was a hill in the distance, and someone was running quickly down it, in the direction of Bracken Hill Town.

'That person's in a hurry!' said Flip, watching him. 'I wonder who he is!'

Flip wouldn't have stayed quietly on the roof if he *had* known who it was. It was Brock Badger hurrying to his cousin Binnie's house to explain how it was he hadn't been to sweep the chimneys as he had promised. He had been looking for his lost brushes all morning!

Brock Badger hurried down the street and at last reached Binnie's big house. He went in at the back way and found Binnie in her kitchen helping her housekeeper mouse to do some washing.

'Well, Brock Badger!' she exclaimed. *'This is a fine time of the day to come!* Wait until I put this pan of water on the fire to boil, and then I'll hear what you've got to say.'

She and the little mouse put the heavy pan of water on the fire. Then Binnie turned to Brock.

'My brushes were stolen!' he said. 'That's why I couldn't come. But I'll do your chimneys when I get them back, Binnie.'

'It's too late,' said Binnie. 'I've got two sweeps now, doing them. They're in the sitting-room.'

Binkle was certainly in the sitting-room, still fitting on poles; but Flip was where we left him, up on the roof. He had become very tired of waiting for the brush to appear.

'I'll just peep down one or two chimneys and see if I can see it anywhere,' he decided.

The chimneys were so tall that he had to climb up them before he could look down. He had just climbed up to look in a pair of chimneys, when something dreadful happened!

The brush suddenly jerked out of the one he was balancing himself on, and pushed him head-foremost down the one he was looking into!

Poor Flip! Down the chimney he went, into the sooty darkness, trying to catch at something to stop himself. But he couldn't – and then SPLASH!

He had fallen straight into the pan of water that Binnie had put on the kitchen fire!

Splutter-splutter! What a to-do there was! Binnie and the little mouse shrieked and ran behind the door. Brock jumped up in amazement and hauled poor choking Flip out of the pan.

'What do you mean by this?' he demanded sternly. 'You're paid to *sweep* chimneys, not to fall down them like that!'

Flip blinked his eyes open and saw Brock!

'Oh! Oh!' he cried, thinking Brock had found out that he and Binkle had stolen his brushes. 'Forgive us, Brock! We didn't mean to take your brushes!'

'Oh! Oh!' said Brock, taking hold of Flip by the scruff of his neck. 'So it was you two, was it? Where's Binkle? In the sitting-room, I suppose!'

Now, Binkle had heard this to-do in the kitchen, and, creeping out, he had seen poor Flip captured. He knew he would be caught next, so he determined to run whilst he had the chance.

He raced out of the front door – straight into the arms of Wily Weasel, the policeman!

Mary Mole was with him.

When she found what a dreadful mess the two sweeps had left in her house, she went straight to Wily and told him. He promised to find the scamps for her, and just as they were walking down the road, making enquiries, Mary had seen the brush sticking out of Binnie's chimney-pot!

So of course she and Wily rushed up to the front door just in time to catch Binkle!

The two bad rabbits cried and said they were terribly sorry – but Wily said he knew their wicked ways and he took them off to lock them up.

He gave them a good scolding, and made them clean Mary Mole's house from top to bottom. Then he gave them another scolding, just for luck, and sent them off.

'We *will* be good now!' said Flip sorrowfully.

'Yes – till the next time you're naughty!' said Wily Weasel with a grunt.

And he was just about right!

Chapter 4

The Wonderful Doctor

Binkle and Flip were just finishing their breakfast, when the postman came.

Rat-a-tat!

'Goodness! That's the postman!' cried Binkle. 'A letter for us – fancy that! I don't believe we've had one for a year.'

He ran to the front door and picked up the letter that lay on the mat.

> *Binkle Bunny,*
> *Heather Cottage,*
> *Bumble Bee Common,*

was the address on the envelope.

'How exciting!' said Flip, when Binkle came running back with the letter. 'Who's it from?'

Binkle opened it. It was not a very long letter.
'Listen!' he said. 'It's from my uncle, Rob
the Rabbit. He keeps a chemist's shop in Oak
Tree Town, just opposite Sammy Squirrel's.'
Then he began to read the letter.

Dear Binkle (it said),
    I have not been well and I must go away for
some time. I know you want work. Would you like
to come and look after my shop whilst I am away?
Then I need not shut it up. Let me know soon.
    Your loving
    Uncle Rob.

Flip and Binkle looked at one another. Then
Binkle stood up and twirled his fine whiskers.
'Ho! Ho!' he said. 'Yes, I'll look after your
shop for you, Uncle Rob. Binkle and Flip
selling medicine and pills! My word, what
fun! What do you say to the idea, Flip?'
'Can we sell medicine and pills properly?'
asked Flip nervously. 'We've never done it
before, you know. I shouldn't like to get into
trouble over it. We always seem to be getting
into trouble somehow.'
'Well, we get out of it too,' said Binkle.
'Don't be so timid, Flip! Come on! Let's make
ourselves tidy, and go and see Uncle Rob.'

65

So the two rabbits washed and cleaned themselves, mended the holes in their socks, patched up their trousers, put on clean ties, rubbed up their hats, and then marched out over Bumble Bee Common looking very spruce and tidy indeed.

They went down Hazel Road till they reached Oak Tree Town. Then they went straight to Rob the Rabbit's shop. It was shut and the blinds were down.

Binkle knocked at the door. Rob Rabbit opened it.

'Come in,' he wheezed. 'I'm glad to see you.'

Binkle and Flip walked in and sat down.

'We got your letter,' said Binkle, 'and we've come to say we'll be pleased to look after your shop till you come back. What's the matter with you?'

'I've got a dreadful cold,' said Rob Rabbit, coughing, 'and it won't go away. So I'm going to stay with my cousin, Bibs Bunny, till it's better.'

Binkle looked round the shop. He saw a great array of bottles, boxes and jars. On one bottle he read:

'Buy this! It's a certain cure for colds!'

He picked it up.

'Why don't you take some of your own medicine?' he asked curiously. 'Look, it says, "certain cure for colds".'

'Won't cure *mine!*' said Rob shortly. 'Mine's too bad. Now look, and I'll explain things to you.'

He took them round the shop and showed them oils and ointments, pills and powders, medicines and mixtures of all kinds.

'They're quite harmless,' he said, 'so if you *do* make a mistake, it won't much matter. The poisonous medicines I've put away in a cupboard. I can't have you running any risks. Business is bad enough as it is.'

'Oh, is it?' asked Binkle. 'Well, it looks as if Sammy Squirrel's chemist shop was doing well, just opposite.'

'It is,' said Rob Rabbit, with a sigh. 'I'm old-fashioned, I suppose. I can't think of any new ideas like Sammy does!'

'Well, never mind,' said Binkle, who had already got the beginnings of a very fine idea himself. 'Go away, and get better. You can safely leave the business with us, you know.'

So Rob took his bag, said goodbye, and

went to stay with his cousin away in Bracken Hill Town.

Flip and Binkle sat down and looked at each other.

'Now look here, Flip,' said Binkle excitedly. 'I've got a fine idea for making this business go well! All we want is to make people curious so that they'll come in here and buy things.'

'What do you mean?' asked Flip, who was always rather afraid of Binkle's ideas.

'I'm going to wrap you up in a big black cloak and an old hat,' said Binkle, 'and I'm going to sit you down just here at the back of the shop where everyone will see you when they come in.'

'Whatever for?' gasped Flip, in great surprise.

'Why, when people come in for anything, and ask who you are, I'm going to say, "Sh! He's a wonderful doctor. He's just come from a far-off country, where he's been making whiskers grow on folk who've never had any, and tails grow thick and long, and beaks shine like gold."' Binkle grew very excited.

'Well, that is silly,' said Flip decidedly. 'I'm not a doctor, and what's the good of pretending? I couldn't do all those things.'

'No, but I could sell the medicine you make which *might* do all those things,' cried Binkle. 'Oh, don't you see? We'll have our shop crowded full, and old Sammy over there won't have any customers at all!'

'All right,' sighed Flip. 'I'll do what you say.'

Binkle rushed about making all sorts of preparations. He pulled down a big black velvet curtain and draped it round Flip. He found an old hat and put it on his head, pulled forwards over his eyes. Then he sat him on a chair at the back of the shop.

'Now we're nearly ready,' he chuckled. He printed some large labels, and put them in a heap on the counter until he would be ready to use them. He filled a number of bottles with green medicine, then some with red, and some with yellow.

Then he opened the shop door and pulled up the blinds. In the window he put a card which said:

THIS SHOP IS UNDER NEW MANAGEMENT.
COME IN AND SEE.

Everybody who passed by read the card. Herbert Hedgehog was very interested, and so was Dilly Duck. Little Timothy Mouse spelt it out to his mother, and Mowdie Mole stopped to put on her spectacles to read it.

Presently the doorbell clanged and someone came in. It was Creeper Mouse the Postman, with a letter for Rob Rabbit. But directly he caught sight of Flip in his black velvet cloak sitting silently at the back of the shop, he jumped, dropped the letter and fled out of the shop.

'Goodness, Flip,' chuckled Binkle, 'see what you've done!' He peeped out of the door and saw Creeper Mouse talking to Slippy Stoat.

'Yes,' Creeper was saying, 'I'm sure it's a

wizard, or something, sitting at the back of the shop there. You go in and see, Slippy.'

Slippy, who was not afraid of anyone, walked up the street and into the shop. He stared in astonishment at Flip.

'Good morning,' said Binkle, from behind the counter. 'What can I do for you?'

'Who's that?' whispered Slippy, pointing to Flip.

'Him? Oh, he's a powerful doctor, a friend of mine,' explained Binkle. 'He's just back from a far-off country.'

'What's he been doing there?' asked Slippy, staring curiously at Flip.

'Making whiskers grow long on the stoats and weasels, and tails grow thick on the rabbits, and beaks shine like gold on the ducks,' answered Binkle at once.

'My word!' said Slippy, pulling at his own whiskers and staring at Flip again. '*My* whiskers are very poor. Could he make them longer, do you think? Shall I ask him?'

'No, no,' said Binkle hurriedly. 'He can't talk our language. I'll ask him for you.'

He went up to Flip, bowed to him, and said: 'Wirri-worra-worra?'

'Dirri-dorra-dorra,' said Flip, in a deep voice.

71

Binkle turned to Slippy.

'He says the red medicine will be just the thing for your whiskers,' he explained, and reached down a bottle. He pasted on it one of his labels which said:

MEDICINE FOR GROWING

LONG WHISKERS.

'One pound, please,' said Binkle.

Slippy paid him the pound, took the bottle, and went out of the shop, thinking the new doctor must be a marvellous man.

On the way home he met Herbert Hedgehog and Dilly Duck. He told them all about the wonderful doctor, and showed them the bottle of red medicine.

'You'll see me with whiskers a foot long soon,' he said. 'Why don't you go and get something to make your beak shine, Dilly?'

'I will!' said Dilly, and waddled off at once, with Herbert Hedgehog.

When they got to the shop, they both stared with round eyes at Flip, who, feeling comfortable and warm in his velvet cloak, had fallen fast asleep. Binkle was there, though, very wide awake.

'Sh!' he said. 'Don't waken him. He was up all last night making a wonderful new ointment for polishing beaks and prickles!'

'Polishing beaks!' cried Dilly.

'Polishing prickles!' said Herbert Hedgehog, very pleased.

'Here it is!' said Binkle, getting down a jar of green ointment. At that moment Flip woke up and yawned.

Binkle was afraid he would say something without thinking, so he bawled across the shop: 'Wirri-worra-worra?'

'Eh?' said Flip, sitting up in surprise. Then he saw the gaping customers and remembered.

'Birri-borra-borra!' he answered, trying not to giggle, and pulling his hat further over his eyes to hide his face.

'He says the green ointment's the right thing for beaks and prickles!' said Binkle. 'One pound each. It's wonderful stuff.'

Herbert and Dilly paid up gladly, and went off with their jars of ointment, which were labelled:

OINTMENT FOR POLISHING
BEAKS AND PRICKLES.

Well, they told everyone they met about the wonderful doctor in Rob Rabbit's shop. And soon all the folk in Oak Tree Town were talking about him, and the marvellous things he could do.

. Tinkle-tinkle-tinkle, went the shop bell all day long. Gillie Guinea-pig came to ask if the doctor knew of something which would grow her a tail. The doctor said, 'Girri-gorra-gorra,' and Binkle explained that that meant the yellow medicine, taken three times a day, would soon grow a tail. Of course Gillie bought a bottle.

Mowdie Mole asked for whisker-growing medicine. Timothy Mouse wanted something to make his tail longer. Riggles Rat wanted something to make his ears grow the proper shape. They had been bitten badly in a fight and looked very ragged.

Binkle was very busy. He kept saying, 'Wirri-worra-worra,' to Flip, till Flip was quite tired of answering him. Also Flip wanted his dinner, and Binkle had been so busy that he hadn't had time to get any.

When the shop got fuller and fuller, and the bottles of medicine got fewer and fewer, Flip became very tired of pretending. He wished all the people would go away. Silly little Derry Dormouse, what did he want to have longer whiskers for? And Hoppety Hare, what did he want with a large tail? Wasn't his own good enough? This chemist business was very boring. It was all very well for Binkle, he was taking lots of money. It was *dull* to sit all day and have nothing to eat.

Then an idea came to Flip. He would soon get rid of all the people and then he could tell Binkle that he wanted something to eat. He jumped up from his chair, pulled his hat over his nose, and yelled at the top of his voice.

'Dorra-borra-worra-wee! Dorra-borra-worra-wee!'

Derry Dormouse screamed and fled out of the shop. So did Riggles Rat. And after one terrified look at Flip, Hoppety Hare shot through the door and was out of sight in a moment.

'Flip! Flip! Whatever's the matter?' gasped Binkle in amazement. 'You've frightened all the customers away!'

'Good job too!' said Flip crossly. 'I want something to eat. Shut up the shop till tomorrow.'

'Certainly not, just when we're doing so well,' said Binkle.

'All right! But you won't have any wonderful doctor any more,' said Flip, and throwing off his black coat, he walked into the backroom and began to look for food.

Of course Binkle had to shut up the shop then, but as he had only about two bottles of medicine left, it didn't matter much.

'We can make some more tonight,' he said. 'Old Sammy Squirrel over the road hasn't had a single customer today I don't believe.'

So that night Binkle made some more ointments and medicines from the different things in his uncle's cupboards.

'We'll have a fine time tomorrow!' he chuckled. 'You'll have to put on that black velvet curtain again, Flip. You looked splendid!'

And next morning Binkle put the shop in order, arranged all his medicines and jars in neat rows, and put Flip in his chair again, wrapped firmly up in his black cloak. Then he waited for customers.

But none came! Not one!

Binkle was puzzled. He peeped out in to the street. No one was about except Sammy Squirrel over the way.

'What's happened?' wondered Binkle. Then he saw Dilly Duck, who kept the post office next door to Sammy Squirrel's shop, come to the window of her shop, and tap on the pane to attract Sammy's attention. She had her beak tied up in flannel.

Sammy ran in to the post office, and came out again after a few minutes. He walked across to Binkle.

'Do you know what's happened?' he said sternly. 'That green ointment that your wonderful doctor said would make Dilly Duck's beak shine has turned it green!'

'Goodness!' said Binkle, sitting down suddenly. 'A green beak! And, oh dear! I suppose Herbert Hedgehog's prickles will have turned green too!'

Sammy snorted and went out again.

Presently he came back.

'Riggles Rat's ill,' he said, 'and so is Hoppety Hare. Slippy Stoat's whiskers have turned red. Derry Dormouse feels sick. Mowdie Mole couldn't get to sleep all night. It seems to me that everyone you sold medicine to yesterday feels very bad indeed. And as for Herbert's prickles, you should just see them! Green as grass they are! I shouldn't be surprised if Wily Weasel the policeman doesn't come for your wonderful doctor and take him off to prison.'

'Ow!' gawped Flip in fright, as Sammy went out again to make some medicines to give to the sick folk. 'Binkle, I *knew* it was a silly idea to dress up like this! You're always having silly ideas!'

'Oh dear!' groaned Binkle. 'This is most unfortunate. I ought to have been more careful. Anyway, nobody will be poisoned, for Uncle put away all his poisons, I know.'

'Yes, and now everyone will go to Sammy Squirrel and buy all *his* medicines to make them better!' said Flip.

Binkle looked out of the shop door. 'Flip!' he cried in fright. 'Wily Weasel's coming!'

'Oh, my stars!' yelled Flip. He dragged off

the black cloak and hat, threw them into a corner and jumped behind the counter, just as Wily Weasel came marching into the shop.

'Where's that doctor?' demanded Wily in his sternest voice.

'Gone!' said Binkle, shaking with fright. 'He's run away. I think he was a bad doctor!'

'Run away, has he?' growled Wily. 'Well, it's a good thing for him that he *has*. I've come to lock him up for making the folk of Oak Tree Town ill! Let me search the shop first, to make sure that he *has* gone!'

He looked all over the shop, but saw no one but the two trembling rabbits, Flip and

Binkle. He pulled out the black velvet cloak and hat and put them over his arm.

'I won't take *you* to prison,' he said to Binkle, 'though you deserve to go. But I think you only did what that bad doctor told you to. But I shall take his hat and cloak, and if ever he comes back and wants them, just send him to me, will you?'

'Y-y-y-yes!' stuttered Binkle, very glad indeed to see Wily go away. When he had gone, he turned to Flip and tried to smile.

'Never mind!' he said. 'We've come off very well. We've got all the money, and – Oh dear!'

And, it was 'Oh dear!' For there in the doorway stood Uncle Rob Rabbit, glaring at him.

'What's this I hear of you selling medicine and making Oak Tree Town ill!' he demanded. 'And what's the tale about that doctor? Oh! I know you, Binkle! You dressed up your friend and pretended all sorts of things. Come on; I'm going to give you to Wily Weasel the Policeman!'

'No! no!' begged Binkle. 'Please don't! We've got lots of money for you, Uncle – look!'

Rob Rabbit looked and could hardly believe his eyes.

'Very well,' he said, 'I won't give you away this time. But I'm going to give you both a good scolding to teach you not to play pranks like this any more.'

And he did. And what's more, he gave them a dose of his nastiest medicine too!

'Oh dear! oh dear!' sighed Binkle, as the two rabbits went sadly home. 'I think we'd better be good for a bit now, Flip – don't you?'

But they couldn't be good for very long, as you will soon hear.

Chapter 5

The Fair at Oak Tree Town

'I say, Flip,' cried Binkle, rushing into Heather Cottage in great excitement. 'What do you think is coming to Oak Tree Town?'

'What?' asked Flip.

'A fair!' said Binkle. 'A fair with roundabouts and swings and everything! Won't it be fun!'

'Yes; but we haven't got any money to go on the roundabouts,' said Flip dolefully.

'No, that's a pity,' frowned Binkle, and pulled at his whiskers and rubbed his nose. Suddenly he stopped and his eyes opened wide.

'Flip!' he said. 'Flip!'

'What?' asked Flip crossly. He was trying to read.

'Oh, Flip!' said Binkle again, in a voice of deepest excitement. 'Flip!'

'Stop "Flipping" me!' said Flip, 'and tell me what you want to say.'

'Flip,' said Binkle, 'I've got the most *won*derful idea I've ever had!'

'Then I'd rather you kept it to yourself,' said Flip, hurriedly folding up his newspaper. 'You shouldn't let yourself have ideas, Binkle.'

'Flip, listen!' cried Binkle, catching hold of him and sitting him down plump in his chair again. 'Wouldn't you like to have enough money to go on all the roundabouts and all the swings and see all the side-shows?'

'Rather!' said Flip.

'Well, I'll tell you how we can,' began Binkle. 'You know how folk love to throw balls at things, in a fair, don't you? They *love* throwing at coconuts and things like that.'

'Yes,' said Flip.

'Well, Flip,' said Binkle, 'wouldn't it be lovely if we could somehow have Herbert Hedgehog to throw at? Think how exciting it would be to see if you could throw a ball and get it stuck on one of his prickles!'

'Binkle,' said Flip in horror, 'whatever will you think of next! As if Herbert would ever agree to that, anyhow!'

'No, he wouldn't *agree*,' said Binkle thoughtfully, 'but I might be able to think of some way that didn't need his consent.'

Well, after a few days, Binkle did think of a way, but he was so afraid Flip would refuse to help him that he decided not to tell everything.

'Look here, Flip,' he said, 'I just want you to take a letter to Herbert for me, will you?'

'All right,' said Flip, reaching for his cap. 'Let me read the letter first, Binkle.'

Binkle read it out loud.

'Dear Herbert Hedgehog,
    'As you are one of the most important people of Oak Tree Town, we should be very much obliged if you would come and open our fair for us tomorrow at three o'clock sharp!'

'But I don't see the sense of writing a letter like that!' said Flip in astonishment.

'You wait and see!' grinned Binkle. 'That will be sure to bring Herbert to the fair all dressed up in his best, and with his new gold watch and all!'

84

'Still, I don't see how we –' began Flip; but Binkle sent him scurrying off, telling him to be sure no one saw him putting the letter into Herbert's letter-box.

Well, when Herbert got that letter, wasn't he pleased and proud!

'Oho!' he said to himself, standing all his prickles on end. 'So the fair people want me to open their show for them, do they? What will all Oak Tree Town say to *that*? I must dress up in my very best!'

He did. And very grand he looked. Last of all he put on his lovely new gold watch and chain. Then he looked at himself in the glass and was very pleased indeed with his appearance.

He set off for the fair, wishing that he could meet Sammy Squirrel or Dilly Duck, so that he might see their faces when he told them he was to open the fair.

But all he met were Flip and Binkle Bunny, also on their way to the fair.

'My!' said Binkle, when he caught sight of Herbert. 'My, Herbert! I never saw you so grand before. How fine you look!'

'I'm going to open the fair,' said Herbert importantly, swelling himself out proudly.

'Well, well, well!' said Binkle, holding up his paws, pretending to be most astonished. 'They made a good choice when they asked you, Herbert. I don't know anybody who could do it better.'

Herbert felt very pleased. He began to think Binkle wasn't such a bad fellow after all.

'Come along with me and hear my opening speech,' he said.

'We'd love to,' said Binkle, 'wouldn't we, Flip?'

'Yes,' agreed Flip, who was very much wondering what would happen when Herbert discovered he wasn't going to open the fair after all!

'But you know, Herbert,' said Binkle solemnly, 'you shouldn't have dressed yourself up so grandly, and you *certainly* shouldn't have put on your gold watch.'

'Why not?' asked Herbert in alarm.

'Well, there are always a rough lot of people at the fair,' said Binkle gravely, 'and if they see you dressed up like that, they might think you'd a lot of money on you – and *rob* you!'

'Oh dear!' said Herbert nervously. 'And I've got my new watch on, too. I wish I hadn't come. I think I'll go home.'

'Oh no, don't do that,' cried Binkle, catching hold of his arm. 'If you like, Herbert, Flip and I will stay with you and look after you.'

'Oh, *thank* you!' cried Herbert, thinking that Flip and Binkle were certainly two very nice fellows. 'That will be fine. Well, here we are at the fair.'

They went through the gates, and Herbert stared in astonishment.

'The fair's begun,' he cried. 'Surely I'm not late!'

'We must be,' said Binkle. 'Oh, what a pity, Herbert! Now you can't open the fair.'

Herbert was terribly disappointed.

87

'I'm going to see the head man about it,' he snorted. 'He's no business to ask me to come, and then to open the fair without me.'

But the head man was very rude. He laughed at Herbert, and said he was mad. Then he became angry and told Herbert to go away, or he'd put him into a coconut shy.

Binkle and Flip pulled him away.

'Never mind,' said Binkle. 'And don't say any more, for goodness' sake, Herbert. Else you really will be put into a coconut shy. Some people can be very rough, you know! And, oh dear! It is a pity you came all dressed up like this! I'm so afraid you'll be robbed.'

Herbert clung to Binkle and begged him not to leave him.

'No, I won't,' promised Binkle. 'Come and look round, Herbert.'

He took Herbert by the arm and led him off. Then Binkle did a very strange thing. He frowned and looked crossly at every single person he met. And, of course, *they* frowned back.

Presently Herbert noticed how crossly everyone looked at them.

'Why does everybody frown at us?' he asked in surprise.

'I'm afraid, I'm very much afraid they don't like you,' said Binkle. 'I expect the head man has sent the word round that you are not a nice person.'

Herbert began to shiver with fright. Just then three badgers and two stoats passed by and frowned most fiercely. He shivered even more.

'Here, Flip,' said Binkle suddenly, just look after Herbert for a minute. I'm going to talk to those fellows who've just passed us, and find out what's the matter with them!'

He left Herbert and Flip and ran up to the badgers and stoats.

'Hey, you fellows!' he said, 'would you like to go in for a fine new throwing game?'

'What sort?' asked the badger.

'Well, you see old Herbert Hedgehog there,' said Binkle. 'I believe I can get him to sit down and let you throw potatoes at him to see if you can get them stuck on his prickles!'

The badgers grinned.

'Never heard of that before,' said one. 'How much does he charge?'

'I'll go and ask him,' said Binkle, and ran back to Herbert.

'I asked them why they looked so angrily at us,' he said to Herbert, 'and what do you think they said?'

'What?' asked Herbert and Flip.

'They said they'd never seen such an ugly fellow as you before, and the sight of your face was enough to make the fair a failure,' said Binkle untruthfully. 'I'm very much afraid you're in for a rough time, Herbert. You saw how everybody scowled at you, didn't you?'

Poor Herbert Hedgehog! He shivered and shook, and shook and shivered, and wished heartily that he'd never come to the fair at all.

'What shall I do?' he asked. 'I'd better go home.'

'I shouldn't do that,' said Binkle; 'it would look as if you were running away. No, I know a simpler plan than that.'

'What?' asked Herbert eagerly.

'I'll take you to a quiet seat I know over there,' said Binkle, pointing. 'There's a wall just behind it, and you can sit facing it, pretending to read a newspaper. Then your back will be to the passers-by, and no one will know who you are.'

'They won't bother about my face if they can't see it,' said Herbert, with a sigh. 'All right, I'll do as you say.'

'Take him, Flip,' ordered Binkle, his wicked eyes dancing with delight and his nose going up and down with excitement.

Flip took Herbert off, and sat him down on the seat Binkle had pointed out, facing a wall. He gave him a newspaper, and then turned to see whatever Binkle was doing.

He was talking excitedly to a small crowd of badgers, stoats, and moles.

'Come on,' he said. 'You can have six throws for fifty pence. There he is, sitting over there, waiting for you to throw at him.'

'Ha! ha!' chuckled Miner Mole, polishing his spectacles. 'I'd like a good old throw at Herbert. He told me my cabbages were good for caterpillars but not for anything else, the other day.'

'And he said my beetroots would pass very well as radishes,' grinned a badger. 'Come on, boys, let's have a shot at him! What luck!'

A small crowd moved towards Herbert.

Binkle produced a big basket full of potatoes which he had dug up from his garden that morning and hidden behind a tent, for he had no money to buy balls. From the basket he took a big notice, and balanced it upright against Herbert's seat.

SIX THROWS FIFTY PENCE!
SPIKE A POTATO ON HERBERT!

Then he started the game by throwing a few potatoes at Herbert himself.

Well, the coins began to roll in like anything. Directly Flip saw what was happening, he began giggling, but Binkle stopped him.

'Be quiet, Flip!' he whispered fiercely. 'You've got to keep Herbert still and pick up the potatoes. Pretend you're throwing them back! You can throw them to me and I'll put them in the basket.'

WHIZZ! WHIZZ! WHIZZ!

The potatoes began spinning through the air, and Herbert gave a tremendous yell of fright and almost fell off his seat.

'It's all right! Keep still!' said Flip. 'Your prickles will protect you, Herbert. I'll pick up the potatoes and throw them back, and keep the fellows off. Don't you worry!'

But Herbert *did* worry. He groaned, grunted, and yelled terrifically whenever a potato stuck on one of his prickles.

The crowd was delighted. Everyone thought Herbert was making a noise to amuse them, and more and more folk came up to join in the fun. The potatoes whizzed merrily through the air and stuck on Herbert, or burst into a score of pieces on the wall behind and spattered into poor Herbert's face. Flip picked up the whole ones and threw them back to Binkle as fast as he could.

'Don't you fret, Herbert,' he panted. 'I'm keeping them off all right.'

Soon half Oak Tree Town came to join in the fun. Dilly Duck and Sammy Squirrel and Brock Badger joined in, and laughed till tears ran from their eyes, to hear Herbert grunting and groaning.

Then Binkle caught sight of Wily Weasel, Oak Tree Town's policeman. At first he was frightened – then an idea came to him.

'Hello, Wily!' he called. 'Six for fifty pence! Have fifty pence worth?'

Now, Wily was a very good shot. He took six potatoes, stood back, and threw them quickly one after the other at Herbert.

Every single one stuck on Herbert's prickles.

But that was too much for Herbert. With a fierce howl of rage he swung himself off the seat, and faced Wily, who had just bought another six and was preparing to throw.

Herbert stared in amazement at Wily.

'Wily!' he gasped. 'Wily Weasel the Policeman! Why didn't you rescue me instead of joining these fellows? And Dilly! And Brock! and Sammy! How can you all stand by and see me treated like this! Gr-rrrrrrf!'

He suddenly picked up a handful of

potatoes and flung them hard at Wily and
Sammy. Wily leapt across to Herbert and took
hold of him angrily.

'Come on, Flip!' whispered Binkle. 'Now's
the time for us to go!'

The two bad bunnies slipped away from the
crowd.

Wily was trying to stop Herbert from
throwing potatoes at everyone, when
suddenly Herbert caught sight of the notice
Binkle had put by his seat. He stared as if he
couldn't believe his eyes.

'Oh! oh! oh!' he wailed suddenly. 'Six
throws for fifty pence! It's all a trick – all a
trick! Quick, Wily, catch Flip and Binkle.'

But Wily wouldn't till Herbert had
explained everything.

Then he began to laugh.

'Oh, Herbert!' he cried, wiping his eyes.
'You'll be the death of me one day! You
shouldn't be such a silly! Fancy letting
yourself be thrown at like that! You might
have guessed Flip and Binkle were up to
mischief.'

'Go and fetch them and scold them!' raged
Herbert. 'Go on, Wily! They've got lots of fifty
pences, all because of me.'

Well, in the end Wily did fetch them. He brought them to Herbert, who glared at them fiercely, and growled.

'Don't, Herbert!' begged Wily. 'You remind me of when you sat on that seat growling, whilst I threw six potatoes at you – and they all stuck!'

'Scold Flip and Binkle!' ordered Herbert. 'They've no business to make money out of me like that!'

Now, Binkle hated being scolded. An idea came to him.

'I'll give you half the money, Herbert,' he said, 'if you'll let us off being scolded. We've got a whole bagful.'

Herbert's little eyes shone. He loved money.

'All right,' he agreed at last. 'Give me half – but mind, you've been let off very easily!'

As Flip and Binkle went off to the roundabouts, Binkle chuckled.

'We *were* let off easily,' he said. 'We didn't deserve to be, either!'

And they certainly didn't – did they?